Hull Terrell

Was Shakespeare a lawyer?

Being a selection of passages

Hull Terrell

Was Shakespeare a lawyer?
Being a selection of passages

ISBN/EAN: 9783337143213

Printed in Europe, USA, Canada, Australia, Japan

Cover: Foto ©Andreas Hilbeck / pixelio.de

More available books at **www.hansebooks.com**

WAS SHAKESPEARE A LAWYER?

BEING A SELECTION OF PASSAGES FROM

"MEASURE FOR MEASURE"

AND

"ALL'S WELL THAT ENDS WELL:"

WHICH POINT TO THE CONCLUSION THAT THEIR AUTHOR MUST HAVE BEEN A PRACTICAL LAWYER; AND IN WHICH MANY OBSCURITIES ARE MADE CLEAR, AND SOME APPARENT CORRUPTIONS IN THE TEXT ARE ATTEMPTED TO BE RESTORED BY AN APPLICATION OF A KNOWLEDGE OF ENGLISH LAW.

By H. T.

LONDON:
LONGMANS, GREEN, READER, AND DYER.
1871.

LONDON:
PRINTED BY WITHERBY & Co.,
MIDDLE ROW PLACE, HOLBORN.

TO

THE RIGHT HONOURABLE LORD HATHERLEY,

LORD HIGH CHANCELLOR OF GREAT BRITAIN,

ETC., ETC., ETC.,

THIS LITTLE BOOK OF LEGAL COMMENTS ON

SHAKESPEARE

IS RESPECTFULLY DEDICATED

BY

HIS LORDSHIP'S OBEDIENT AND HUMBLE SERVANT

THE AUTHOR.

London, January, 1871.

WAS SHAKESPEARE A LAWYER?

THE pages of Shakespeare's Plays are allowed to be strewed with references to English laws; but, on a careful examination, we have found that such references are far more numerous than has been usually supposed. In fact, the Poet's memory appears to have been full to overflowing of the principles and practice of Law, and of the quibbles and technicalities of the legal profession. Hence an interesting question has been raised as to whether Shakespeare had ever been engaged in the study or practice of English law. A little book on this subject was published by the late Lord Chancellor Campbell. In it his Lordship gave the results of his examination of twenty-three, out of the thirty-seven, Plays which have been ascribed to our Great Dramatist. His judgment, delivered with the proverbial caution of a Scotchman, was, that no positive answer could be given to the question. We venture to think, however, that the trial was not satisfactorily conducted, in that the investigation was too cursorily made. His Lordship noted only such passages as, without study, would have suggested themselves even to a non-legal mind; whilst others were passed by. He has not condescended to point out the minuter phenomena—in the colouring which narrations take during their passage through a legal mind, in the constant verbal wrangling begotten by legal logic, and in the practice of splitting words into double or treble senses. Indeed, his Lordship states that his object was, rather to throw out *hints* which might be useful to others who should pursue the same line of inquiry, than fully to work out his problem. There is, therefore, a demand for a new trial, which, we think, may be carried on more searchingly by a fuller examination of the evidence.

There are seven years in the early life of Shakespeare, being a part of the period of his presumed residence at Stratford, which have not been accounted for by his biographers. Nothing has been hitherto produced to show how these years were employed. It is probable, from the depressed state of his father's pecuniary affairs, that his son William was earning his own livelihood; and no reason can be shown against his having been employed as a clerk in an attorney's office: and it does not seem to be probable that such an occupation would have been distasteful to his mental constitution. The practice of a lawyer's chambers would have admitted him behind the scenes in many worldly proceedings, and have enabled him to see the distinction between motive and pretence, and between law and justice. From "Hudibras" we perceive how a drama may be acted in an advising lawyer's presence. From such a limited stage Shakespeare may have learnt how great results often spring from mere misunderstandings, in which both the parties interested are innocent of evil intentions; and how, under the overruling influence of circumstances, wrong may, for a period, prevail against the right, and vice might often strangle virtue. Supposing that Shakespeare was ever a clerk to an attorney, the whole of the legal lore which may be gathered from his Plays can be accounted for satisfactorily.

In opposition to this hypothesis are two others. The one is, that Shakespeare, after he came to London, might have been more than ordinarily addicted to the attending of courts of justice, where he might have picked up his legal notions, and have learnt the use of legal jargon. The supreme courts were arranged, in his time, around the inner walls of Westminster Hall, and in the neighbourhood of petty stalls of traffickers, so that the Hall became attractive to the public, and detained the idle lounger by the hour. A second is that which is stated by Dr. Bucknill, in his elegant inquiry into "the Medical Knowledge of Shakespeare." The Doctor deems that the Poet's father having been engaged in legal transactions, the son might have gleaned many technicalities, which his infallible memory would afterwards have reproduced.

To both objections there is one reply : that any practising lawyer, who had *attentively* studied the Plays, would feel satisfied that neither of such supposed sources of professional knowledge would be sufficient to account for the perpetual and abundant crop of legal lore which bristles over the productions of Shakespeare's mind. But to this it may be answered, that the introduction of so much law into a play would imply that an equal acquaintance with the niceties of law was common to all people ; for otherwise the actors would have been unintelligible to the popular part of their audience. Now this objection to our hypothesis would seem to be unanswerable, unless we considered—first, that authors often introduce words and matters into their compositions with which they themselves are most familiar ; and also, secondly, in reference to Shakespeare, this special circumstance—that the lawyers of the day were his great patrons. Some of his Plays even read as if they had been composed to have been acted before a legal audience ; and, as the Poet would desire to please his hearers on the floor by throwing to them low, and often the coarsest bits of buffoonery ; so he might be allowed to try to delight his legal hearers in the balcony, by some scrapes on their professional fiddle.

A sensible observation was made by one of our greatest literary critics applicable to the case of Shakespeare ; and confirmatory of the hypothesis, that our Dramatist was early initiated into the mysteries of English law. S. T. Coleridge remarked, that an author's observations of life would be drawn from the immediate employments of his youth, and from the character and images most deeply impressed on his mind, and the situation in which these employments had placed him. He gave two illustrations, viz., Ben Jonson the soldier, who introduced soldiers and their peculiarities into his plays ; and Lessing the university-man, who has made us familiar with the scenes of academic life. What was true of Ben Jonson and of Lessing, was probably equally true of Shakespeare. Anyhow, it is characteristic of human nature that the apprentice should carry about with him in after life a vivid remembrance of the shop.

Two other general observations may be made on the internal evidence of Shakespeare's connection with the legal profession. The first shows that he was well acquainted with law, inasmuch as that, when he allows any of his characters to speak law, they not being professional lawyers, he makes them talk nonsense. In this he evinces a professional pride—a sentiment which is common to men of all professions; hence non-professionals are allowed to lay down bad law and to misuse legal words. On the contrary, when his lawyers speak, their doctrine is always sound, and their technical terms are correct; so that the Dramas of the Poet might find their place on the shelves of a library by the side of my Lord Coke.

The second peculiarity indicates that Shakespeare had been in an attorney's office. The Poet often speaks disparagingly of judges; he makes fun of Justices of the Peace (the Lucys) ; and he held in low respect all the officers connected with courts of justice. This being the case, it is to be noted that he is ever careful of the character of attornies. We think that he was no naughty bird. And yet the class of attornies have long been the but of wits and witlings. Had Shakespeare lived in our day, he might even have praised them, and have joined in the reported words of a Vice-Chancellor concerning solicitors : " I am bound to say of the great body of solicitors that a more honourable set of men does not exist." Yet we do not remember that any Act of Parliament has been ever passed, conferring substantial advantages on attornies or solicitors; nor have they any honorary steps in their profession—not even the military sham of the coveted brevet rank.

We now propose to make a critical examination of two of Shakespeare's Plays, viz., " Measure for Measure " and "All's Well that Ends Well," for the purpose of ascertaining whether their author had studied law, and been a practical lawyer; at the same time to notice how many obscure passages can be made clear, and how many corruptions of the text may be restored, by an application of a knowledge of that system of law with which we have supposed that our Poet had become well acquainted.

It is to be remarked, concerning the quotations to be pre-sented in illustration of the hypothesis that Shakespeare was a lawyer—

1. That some of them point to a special acquaintance with English law and its technicalities, such as could be expected only from an intelligent legal practitioner.

2. That others suggest an unusual familiarity with legal notions and customs, the reference to which is as a second nature with Lawyers, as texts of Scripture are with Divines.

3. That many passages show an ignorance of law terms in the printers; and these it is proposed to correct by substituting sense for nonsense.

4. That in some of the passages which *primâ facie* show cor-ruption, we have ventured to suggest what was their original condition, in confirmation of the admitted presumption that the MSS. used by the first printers were often unintelligible to them, whereby the printed texts were so defaced as to invite to a friendly though respectful correction of them.

"MEASURE FOR MEASURE."

This Play is especially suited to our purpose; for it exhibits even to detail, judges, parties, pleaders, witnesses, jailers, and exe-cutioners, as they appeared and acted in Shakespeare's time. It is scarcely probable that any writer, who was not intimately acquainted with English legal proceedings, would have ventured to tread upon such ground. Until within a few years past, writers of fiction usually abstained from the misty labyrinths of the law, lest they should be in danger of overhearing a laugh. Miss Edgworth once ventured on this sacred domain, and, as a result, her plaintiffs and defendants dance in glorious confusion on her pages.

In this play of "Measure for Measure," Lord Campbell noted only *four* passages as indicating Shakespeare's knowledge of law:

they are, Act I., Scene 2, "Good councillors lack no clients;" Act II., Scene 1, "Action of battery and slander;" Act II., Scene 2, "Your brother is a forfeit of the law;" and Act III., Scene 2, in which the judges call each other "brother." How perfunctorily, and therefore unsatisfactorily, his Lordship performed his office of a legal commentator, we shall endeavour to show.

ACT I., SCENE 1.

1.   "DUKE (to *Escalus*). The nature of our people,
   Our city's institutions, and the *terms*
   For *common justice*, you're as pregnant in.
   .   .   . There is our *commission*."

In these four lines we meet with three legal technicalities. In "the terms for common justice," *terms* does not refer to words, but to times—the legal year being divided into four terms, with intervening vacations. "Common justice" has a reference to the "Court of Common Pleas." A "commission" was a legal expression for a delegation of certain powers by a sovereign for a certain end. The judges on circuit, as Shakespeare must have known, acted under royal commissions of *oyer and terminer—i.e.*, to hear and decide disputes.

2.   "DUKE (to *Escalus*). We have with special *soul*
   Elected him [Angelo] our absence to supply;
   Lent him our terror, *drest* him with our *love*."

For "soul" we propose to read *zeal*, and for "love," *lore*. In "drest him" we have perhaps a reference to a legal fiction that a judge's robe always covered a lawyer. Robes of office seem to have a strong effect on Shakespeare's mind, as we shall see that he often refers to them.

In English law judges have by fiction a kind of infallibility thrown around them. A party suffering by their mistake or delay is without a remedy. This irresponsibility speaks in favour of our judges. According to the law of Norway, if a party is dissatisfied with the judgment given from the Bench, he may bring an action against the judge; and instances are recorded in which very large damages have been given against the offenders.

3. " DUKE (to *Angelo*). Nature never *lends*
    The smallest scruple of her excellence,
    But, like a thrifty goddess, she determines
    Herself the *glory* of a creditor,
    Both thanks and *use*."

" Nature " is here introduced under the legal aspect of a scrivener, usually a lawyer, prescribing to her creditor conditions of repayment of a loan. " Use " is an old legal term for interest. The meaning of "glory" is scarcely perceptible : the *duty* of a creditor would be more intelligible.

4. " DUKE (to *Angelo*). Hold, therefore, Angelo ! [handing him the commission].
    In our remove, be thou at full *ourself*:
    .   .   .   . Old Escalus,
    Though *first in question*, is thy *secondary*."

The phrase " at full ourself " represents a legal English fiction, according to which the sovereign was always present in court with his judges, notwithstanding his remove or absence. Hence writs issued by a judge were tested " *before ourselves*," *i.e.*, the sovereign. Another phrase here introduced, " though first in question," we must attribute to the printer's ignorance. There is, we think, little doubt but that we ought to read, *though put in quorum*—the reference being to the terms of the commission under which Justices of the Peace were appointed, in which many were named together as justices, yet some were specially enumerated on account of their superior fitness of office ; and of these, *one* at least was required to be present on the Bench when sitting. Hence the expression inserted in the commission, " quorum," *i.e.*, *of whom*, &c. We must not for " secondary " read *secretary*. A " secondary " was a well-known legal officer.

5. " DUKE (to *Angelo* and *Escalus*). To the hopeful *execution*
    do I leave you
    Of your commissions."

The term "execution," though now in common use, was born in Westminster Hall. It means the putting of the law in force—*e.g.*, the hanging of a felon is, in legal parlance, his *execution*.

6. "DUKE (to *Angelo*). Your scope is as mine own :
So to *enforce* and *qualify* the laws
As to your *soul* seems good."

Instead of "soul" we prefer to read *zeal*, as before. By "to enforce and qualify the laws" is meant, that the commissioners were to unite in themselves the power of sentencing, which was the usual duty of a judge ; and also of pardoning, which was the attribute of the sovereign alone. As the English law knew of no precedent for the combination of such powers, our princes having ceased to act personally as judges, Shakespeare does not introduce any English legal terms, which would only mislead. Such a restraint shows a knowledge of the technicalities of our laws.

7. "ESCALUS (to *Angelo*). I shall desire you, Sir, to give me leave to have free speech with you ; and it concerns me to look into *the bottom of my place*.
A power I have ; but of what strength and nature I am not yet instructed."

We have "in the bottom of my place" a phrase which is neither poetical nor elegant. Escalus is addressing his superior, Angelo. Was the Poet thinking of the mark of pre-eminence enjoyed by the Lord Chancellor, as the head of the legal body, in that he rested on the *woolsack*, whilst the other judges sat on *benches ?* Such a distinction might raise a smile from a Templar.

SCENE 2.

8. "LUCIO. If the Duke, with the other Dukes, *come not to composition* with the King of Hungary, why, then all the Dukes fall upon the King."

An ordinary writer would have said, *Come not to an arrangement*, or agreement ; but Shakespeare prefers to introduce the technical term "composition," *i.e.*, a *decisio litis*. The expression is far-fetched; but then Lucio was not a lawyer, but "a fantastic."

SCENE 3.

9. "CLAUDIO (to *Provost*). Fellow, why dost thou show me
thus to the world?
Bear me to prison, where I am committed.
PROVOST. I do it not in evil disposition,
But from Lord Angelo by special charge.
CLAUDIO. Thus can the demi-god, Authority,
Make us pay down for our offence *by weight*."

Claudio having been arrested by the Provost, and being *led* publicly through the streets, complains and asks to be *carried* to prison, which seems to have been the custom. The remembrance of this still survives in the phrase "carried to prison." Instead of "by weight" we prefer to read "by right," *i.e.*, Lord Angelo had authority to vary the custom of commitment to prison, and augment its shame by making the accused walk.

10. "LUCIO. Why, how now, Claudio? whence comes this
restraint?
CLAUDIO. From too much liberty, my Lucio, liberty——
LUCIO. If I could speak so wisely under an *arrest*, I would
send for certain of my *creditors* : And yet, to say the truth,
I had as lief have the *foppery* of freedom, as the *morality* of
imprisonment."

For "the morality of imprisonment" we prefer to read *reality of imprisonment*. For "the foppery of freedom" we prefer to read, the *frippery* of freedom. "Frippery" means what is contemptible and trifling: thus, Ben Jonson says, "the frippery of wit." As to sending for "creditors," the meaning is, that they might become bound as bail for the appearance of Claudio afterwards, if he should then be discharged from personal arrest. Creditors are supposed to be very interested parties in getting their debtor out of prison, in order that they might obtain payment afterwards. The meaning of Lucio's speech seems to be, that if he himself had been arrested, he would have endeavoured to avoid imprisonment by procuring bail for his appearance, when required—as he should prefer such temporary personal freedom as could be thus obtained, to the reality of being imprisoned.

11.   "CLAUDIO (to *Lucio*). Thus stands it with me :—Upon a true contráct,

I got possession of Julietta's bed ;
You know the lady ; she *is fast my wife*,
Save that we do the *denunciation* lack
Of outward order : this we came not to,
Only for *propagation* of a dower
Remaining in the coffer of her friends ;
From whom we thought it meet to hide our love,
Till time had made them for us."

In these lines are set forth the laws and customs concerning marriage : but some terms are obscure to the non-legal apprehension ; and there is one corruption which a knowledge of law can, we think, best restore.

According to the canon law, a " true contract " of marriage might be made *privately* between the man and the woman, which was binding on them, although no public ceremonies were added. Such a contract having taken place between Claudio and Juliet, he could say of her, " she is fast my wife." (Conf. Hen.VI., 5, 2). " Denunciation " is an old ecclesiastical term for *proclamation*, as applied to banns of marriage. Instead of " only for propagation of a dower," we should read, *only for procuration of a dower*. The reference is to a custom of paying procuration money to such as could secure for an unmarried man the hand of a rich heiress. Claudio seems to intimate that it was for the purpose of avoiding such a payment that his marriage with Juliet, an heiress, had been kept secret. The passage seems to need some other, though perhaps slight, amendments to make it genuine.

12.   "CLAUDIO. The strength of our most mutual entertainment, With *character* too *gross*, is *writ* on Juliet."

These lines read like the words of a lawyer's clerk. A legal document copied in a thick and distinct style (character), such as was the old English text, was called *engrossed*. A gross character meant, therefore, a plain style of writing. The true meaning of this passage, in a legal sense, is thus obvious; but the expressions are gross in another sense.

13. " CLAUDIO (to *Lucio*). This new governor
Awakes me all the *enrolled penalties*,
Which have, like *unscour'd armour*, hung by the wall
So long, that *nineteen zodiacs* have gone round,
And none of them been worn."

What, it may be asked, was the probable connection in Shakespeare's mind between the " enrolled penalties," the " unscour'd armour hung upon the wall," and " zodiacs ? " We suggest that it was legal scenery. In the park of the Lucy family, near Stratford, stands the old family mansion. Howitt, in his Visits to Remarkable Places, has given a drawing of its lofty and spacious entrance hall. It was probably the residence of the Lord of the Manor, and, if so, the Manor Courts would have been held in the hall; or, Sir Thomas Lucy may have heard complaints in it, as a Justice of the Peace. Let us imagine that Shakespeare had been present before Sir Thomas in defence of some copyholder of the manor, who had incurred some penalty laid down in its records, which are called *Rolls*, and hence " enrolled penalties." Then let us imagine him casting his eyes around the walls of the hall, as he waited for his turn, and he might have seen, as hung there, the old memorials of family military history, armour long " unscoured," because long unused. Then let us imagine that some member of the Lucy race had been engaged in the naval adventures which had attracted so many restless youths during the age of our Poet, and that a "zodiac" stood in a corner as a momento of exploits upon the sea. Now, if such a scene had presented itself to the young lawyer whilst patiently waiting and musing in the hall of justice, we can easily account for the association of ideas which he has put into the mouth of Claudio, and which ideas had never lost their relationship after they had once been stamped upon the Poet's faithful memory.

The number "nineteen," in connection with "zodiacs," or years, seems also to carry a legal idea. Twenty years was in some cases considered in law to be a bar to adverse claims. If so, the argument put into the mouth of Claudio was—that it was hard to bring him under the penalties of a law which, having been allowed to sleep so long a time, would soon have covered his defects. Now, Claudio was not a lawyer ; but, as a grumbler, he might be supposed to have used a popular argument.

SCENE 5.

14.   " ISABELLA.   Doth he [Angelo] so
Seek his [Claudio's] life ?
       LUCIO. Has *censur'd* him already,
       And, as I hear, the Provost has a *warrant*
       For his execution."

We have here two legal terms. " Censured" does not mean *blamed*, but is a term of ecclesiastical law, signifying *condemned*, as appears from the context. After the censuring of Claudio followed the " warrant for his execution."

ACT II., SCENE 1.

15.   " ANGELO (to *Escalus*). The jury, *passing* on the prisoner's
       life,
       May, in the sworn twelve, have a thief or two
       Guiltier than him they try."

" Passing " is a term applicable to the judge who *passes sentence*, and not to the jury. We might therefore prefer, with probability, to read *the jury panneled*, *i.e.*, impanneled *on the prisoner's life*. This twelve were called a *Pannel*. To impannel a jury was to enter their names in a schedule. Thus we have intelligible law.

16.   " ELBOW (to *Angelo*). If it please your honour, I am the poor
       Duke's *constable*, and my name is *Elbow*, and I do *lean* upon
       justice, Sir."

A friend has ingeniously suggested that the constable here per-

petrated a legal pun, when he says that his name is *Elbow*, and that
he *leans* on justice.

17.   "Escalus (to *Elbow*). How do you know that ?
      Elbow. My wife, Sir, whom I *detest* before heaven and
your honour.
      Escalus. How ! thy wife ?
      Elbow. Ay, Sir, whom, I thank heaven, is an honest
woman.
      Escalus. Dost thou *detest* her therefore ?
      Elbow. I say, Sir ; I will *detest* myself also, as well as
she, that this house," &c.

Here Elbow blunders into nonsense by attempting to use a law
term. For "detest" we must read *attest*, *i.e.*, to testify. Elbow,
the constable, appears as an illustration of what has been already
noticed, that Shakespeare makes his non-legal personages, when
they would pretend to know law, convict themselves of presumption
by talking nonsense. Of this another instance follows :—

18.   "Pompey (to *Escalus*). I'll be *supposed* upon a book, his
      face is the worst thing about him."

Pompey is giving evidence before a judge. We should therefore
prefer, instead of "supposed," to read *subpœned upon a book*, *i.e.*,
sworn upon the Gospels. But even then, Pompey, not being a
lawyer, confounds being *subpœned*, which means being summoned
under a penalty (*sub pœnâ*), to attend and give evidence, with being
sworn, before he gave his testimony.

19.   "Pompey (in Court, addressing the *Judge*). By this hand,
      Sir, his wife is a more respected person than any of us all."

By "this hand," which Pompey is to be supposed to hold up, a
reference is made to a form of taking an oath.

20.   "Escalus (addressing *Elbow*). Truly, officer, because he
      hath some *offences in him*, that thou would'st discover if thou
      could'st, let him *continue in his courses* till thou know'st what
      they are."

By this, Escalus, the judge, seems to mean—that as the charges against the prisoner had not been already proved, although he was a suspected person, and had " offences in him," *i.e.*, as yet undiscovered, he was to be dismissed, in order that the constable, Elbow, might keep an eye upon him. On this the constable, addressing the prisoner, and mistaking the meaning of the words used by the judge, says :—

" ELBOW. Marry, I thank your lordship for it."

And then, turning to the prisoner, he says :—

" Thou see'st, thou wicked varlet, now, what's come upon thee ; thou art *to continue now*, thou varlet ; thou art *to continue*" [meaning in custody].

But " to continue," in law, meant often to postpone a case to another term, and did not imply a continuance in custody.

21.   " ESCALUS. Master Froth, I would not have you acquainted with tapsters ; they will *draw* you, Master Froth, and you will *hang* them ; get you gone, and let me hear no more of you."

In giving this good advice, the judge seems to speak playfully, and uses words with a double meaning. The tapsters would *draw* Master Froth, *i.e.*, like a cork, and take his money, and Master Froth, by his evidence, would cause tapsters to be *hanged* for their crime. The words of " drawing " and " hanging," proceeding together from the mouth of a judge on the Bench, carried with them unpleasant associations, and pointed to the gallows at Tyburn.

22.   " ESCALUS. Pompey, you are partly a bawd, Pompey, howsoever you colour it by being a tapster. *Are you not ?* "

Shakespeare here represents a custom of his time in criminal charges, but since changed ; for no attempt can now be made to induce a prisoner to confess and convict himself ; on the contrary, he is warned against so doing.

Scene 2.

23. "ANGELO (to *Isabella*). Mine were the very cipher of a
function,
To fine *the fault, whose fine stands on record,*
And let go by the actor."

Instead of "to fine the fault," it would probably be better to
read, *to fine his fault,* and so to provide an antecedent to "whose."
The words "stands on record" refer to the higher courts of justice,
called Courts of Record, in whose proceedings *fines* due to the
sovereign would be *recorded.*

24. "ISABELLA (to *Angelo*). Why, all the souls that were [qy.
are], were *forfeit* once ;
And he that might the *vantage* best have took
Found out the *remedy.*"

We have here a doctrine of Western theology, which was based
on Roman jurisprudence, and is expressed in forensic terms.—(*Vide*
Maines' *Ancient Law.*)

25. "ANGELO (to *Isabella*). It is the law, not I, that condemns
your brother."

This distinction is always made by our criminal judges, who,
avoiding all personal feeling and responsibility, are content to say,
"The sentence of the law is so-and-so." The dignity and impar-
tiality of our English judges contrast favourably with the conduct
of judges in some countries. Perhaps the only case in which an
English judge in a criminal court is allowed to show the *man,* is
when duty calls on him to pronounce the extreme sentence of the
law, which is usually accompanied by an exhortation to repentance,
and a prayer. Our judicial body are, probably, of all state officers,
the class to which an Englishman would point a foreigner with the
most unqualified approbation for unimpeachable fulfilment of duty,
and freedom from suspicion of partiality.

26.   "ANGELO (to *Isabella*). The law hath not been dead,
though it hath slept.

.   .   .   .   . now 'tis awake ;
Takes note of what is done ; and, like a prophet,
Looks in a glass, that shows what future evils
Are now to have no *successive degrees*,
But ere they live, to end."

The phrase "no successive degrees" is borrowed from law, and refers to inheritances passing to the son from the father. Angelo means that existing evils should not be propagated, *i.e.*, Claudio should die for his crime and not live to be imitated by any children.

SCENE 3

27.   "DUKE (as a Friar, to *Juliet*). I'll teach you how you
shall *arraign* your conscience,
And *try* your penitence, if it be sound,
Or hollowly put on."

Even the Duke, although he has assumed the garb of a friar, has legal words put into his mouth. "To arraign" and "try" are law terms. The former refers to a prisoner's being placed at the bar to answer guilty or not guilty, previous to his being *tried*. Shakespeare sometimes uses theological terms, though he often makes direct references to, and quotations from the Sacred Scriptures.

28.   "JULIET (to the *Duke*, as a Friar). I do confess it, and
repent it, father.
DUKE. 'Tis meet, my daughter ; *but lest* you do repent,
As that *the* sin has brought you to this shame."

This passage is obscure, as the *name* of "the sin" is omitted. May it be restored thus ?—

'Tis meet, my daughter, *that lust* you do repent,
In that *this* sin has brought you to this shame.

If these suggestions are approved, they throw light on what immediately follows :—

" DUKE (*continuing*). *Which sorrow* is always towards our-
    selves, not heaven ;
Showing we would not spare *heaven*, as we love it,
But as we stand in fear."

For " which sorrow " we would propose to read *world-sorrow*,
thus taking " world " as standing in opposition to " heaven."

SCENE 4.

29.   " ANGELO.   The *state*, whereon I *studied*,
  Is like a good thing, being often read,
  Grown sear'd and tedious."

This passage seems, *primâ facie*, to have a reference to legal studies,
but not so, if it is read as we think it originally stood, and insert
" steadied " for " studied." The meaning would then be—that
Angelo having relied on his state or dignity as deputy to the Duke,
the use of it had made him weary, and a respect for it had become
tedious, so that it did not keep him from falling into temptation.

30.   " ANGELO (to *Isabella*). Their saucy sweetness, that do
    coin heaven's image
  In *stamps* that are forbid."

The judge here compares the begetting of illegitimate children to
the *crime* of making false coin and stamping it with the sovereign's
image.

31.   " ANGELO (to *Isabella*.) I talk not of your soul : our
    compell'd sins
  Stand more for number than for accompt.
  ISABELLA.   How say you ?
  ANGELO. Nay, I'll not warrant that, for *I can speak*
  Against the thing I say."

Here Angelo, having turned special pleader, makes a distinction
between two kinds of sins, the correctness of which Isabella ques-
tions. In reply to her, Angelo retracts what he had said, and makes
a second distinction, probably not sounder than his first. It is this :

that an advocate might say, as an advocate, what he would not say as a man—a license sometimes claimed by English barristers, though always repudiated by them in practice when they become judges.

32.   "ANGELO (to *Isabella*). I, now the *voice* of the recorded law.' Pronounce a sentence on your brother's *life*."

Shakespeare has here caught the true spirit of our English courts of criminal justice.   It is not the judge who pronounces the sentence, but "the voice of the recorded law."   Again, the sentence is not against the man, but his "life."   Justice with us wears the air of an Abstraction, and the impersonality of a Necessity.

33.   "ANGELO (to *Isabella*). And his offence is so, as it appears, *Accountant* to the law upon that *pain*."

"Accountant" is here used figuratively.   The offender is supposed to *owe* something to the law, which demands something on the credit side.   "Pain" is a legal term, derived from the Norman-French *peine*, and is equivalent to penalty.

34.   "ANGELO (to *Isabella*). Admit no other way to save his life,—
      As I subscribe not that, nor any other,
      But in the *loss of question*."

"The loss of question" reads like nonsense.   If we were to make an alteration, which would be in something less than a single letter, and read *the toss of question*, we may suppose that the Poet had in his mind a method sometimes adopted by jurors to settle a difference of opinion amongst them, viz., by a toss-up.

35.   "ANGELO (to *Isabella*). We all are frail
          ISABELLA.   Else let my brother die,
      If not a foedary, but only he
      Owe, and succeed thy weakness.
          ANGELO. Nay, women are frail too.
          ISABELLA. Women! help heaven! Men their creation mar
      In profiting by them. Nay, call us ten times frail."

We have here a very corrupt text, and such as might puzzle a sphinx. The metre is faulty, so that something may have been added or omitted. The argument being apparently based on law, the law may lead us some way in understanding the Poet. "Fœdary" is not an English word, but *federary* is, and is used elsewhere by Shakespeare in the sense of confederate in crime. The argument might be supposed to run thus:—Angelo says to Isabella, "We all are frail," to which she replies, "Else let my brother die," meaning if he alone had sinned as he had; and she adds, in explanation, "if not a 'federary,'" in sinning with others also. She then seems to turn to Angelo, with an *argumentum ad hominem*, suggesting her brother had only *succeeded* (used elsewhere in the sense of *followed*) the weakness shown by Angelo himself. Angelo, disliking this thrust at himself, turns the subject, and accuses Isabella as one of a class, saying, "Nay, women are frail too." This Isabella meets by a confession on the part of her sex, and by a recrimination on the male sex. We have here, apparently, the legal shuffling of the lawyer Angelo, refuted by the straightforwardness of the saintly Isabella.

36.   "ANGELO (to *Isabella*). I do *arrest* your words."

By which he means, I hold you to your admission that "women are frail." Then follow these obscure lines from Angelo:—

> "Be that you are,
> That is, a woman, ...
> as you have well expressed
> By all external warrants,—shew it now,
> By putting *on* the *destined livery*."

The apparently close connection between "putting on" and "livery" might lead to the conclusion that Shakespeare was here speaking of dress; but then the line is inexplicable. What "livery" could Angelo mean? If, however, for "putting on" we read *putting off*; and if we take "livery" for *delivery*, in the legal sense, as in the phrase *livery of seisen, i.e.*, delivery of possession, Angelo's argument may be:—You admit that women are frail,—you are a woman; shew yourself such by submitting to my will, and so *putting off the destined delivery, i.e.*, of your brother to death, as a punishment for his offence. *Destined delivery* would have destroyed both euphony and metre, while "livery" saves both.

37.   "ISABELLA (to *Angelo*).   O perilous mouths,
That bear in them one and the self-same tongue,
Either of condemnation or *approof.*"

We are not here to understand by "approof" *approval.* It has a legal technical meaning. An *approver* was one who confessed a participation in a crime, and then turned against his confederate, or "foedary," as Shakespeare had just before employed this term. The term "approof" is here most aptly introduced, and with its right legal meaning.

ACT III., SCENE 1.

38.   "ISABELLA (to *Claudio*). This outward-sainted deputy,—
Whose settled visage and deliberate word
Nips youth i' the head and follies [qr. feathers], doth enmew,
As falcon doth the fowl,—is yet a devil;
His filth within being cast, he would appear
A pond as deep as hell.
            CLAUDIO.   The *prenzie* Angelo!
            ISABELLA. O, 'tis the cunning *livery* of hell,
The damned'st body to *invest* and *cover*
In *prenzie* guards!"

The word "prenzie," here twice repeated according to the first folio, has been a *crux* to commentators. It is admittedly a misprint —but for what? Priestly, princely, precise, venerable, and, according to Mr. Staunton, "reverend," are specimens of the corrections which have been suggested; but neither has been shown to have any special appropriateness to Angelo: and Shakespeare is not guilty of inserting mere empty epithets. Angelo is being spoken of as deputy and judge, and we think that two small corrections will remove all difficulties from the passage, which, it seems, turns on legal robes and dignity. For "guards" we propose to read *gauds, i.e.*, the external ornaments of the judge's person—a word often used by Shakespeare;

and for "prenzie" we would read *frippery*—a term elsewhere used by the Poet in the sense of borrowed, or second-hand, as applied to clothes. A dealer in old clothes was called a fripper. The word has this meaning attached to it in the *Liber Albus* of the City of London. In "The Tempest" we read—

> "TRINCULO. O King Stephano! O peer! O worthy Stephano! look what a *wardrobe* is for thee.
> CALIBAN. Let it alone, thou fool; it is but *trash*.
> TRINCULO. O, he, monster! we know what belongs to a *frippery*.
> STEPHANO. Put off that *gown*, Trinculo."

Now, assuming the propriety of the two corrections which we propose to make in the text, the argument of the passage will run thus:—Isabella had been charging, before her brother Claudio, Angelo, the deputy of the absent Duke, with hypocrisy, for intending to punish her brother Claudio for an offence similar to that which he himself desired to commit with herself. She calls him "this outward-sainted deputy," and adds, "is yet a devil," thereby making prominent two facts—First, that he was but a deputy of the Duke, though wearing judges' robes; and, secondly, that his assumption of external dignity did not correspond with his inner man. When Isabella lays before Claudio these facts, he interrupts her by expressed contempt for Angelo, exclaiming, "The frippery Angelo;" thus, in two words, adapting Isabella's expressed opinion of Angelo. Claudio having thus introduced the idea of dress, Isabella takes it up, and says:—

> " O, 'tis the cunning *livery* of hell,
> The damned'st body to *invest* and *cover*
> In frippery *gauds*," [*i.e.*, in mere Deputy's robes.]

It is to be noted, that in six other passages in his Plays Shakespeare introduces the ideas of office, shame, and dress, in connection with each other, *e.g.* :—

> " ISABELLA.   Even so may Angelo,
> In all his dressings, characts, titles, forms,
> Be an arch villain."   (ACT V., SCENE 1.)

ACT III., SCENE 1.

39. "DUKE (to *Isabella*). By this, is your brother saved, your honour untainted, the poor Mariana avenged, and the corrupt Deputy *scaled*."

For "scaled" we propose, as before, to read *sealed*. In law a seal gave increased value to a document. In Act V., Scene 1, we read, "That's sealed in approbation." The Duke had just before told Isabella that her evidence against Angelo would be insufficient, and he now proposed a plan which would *seal* his criminality, *i.e.*, make it undoubted.

SCENE 2.

40. "ESCALUS. Provost, *my brother* Angelo will not be altered."

Here Escalus calls Angelo, "my brother." The judges in West-minster Hall still call each other "brother." All these judges first become serjeants. The serjeants were originally clerics, and so called each other *brother*. The black patch on the wig represents the coif, or shaving on the top of the head. It may be, that the custom for the judge to put on the black cap when he pronounces sentence of death, was originally intended to conceal the symbol of his being of the clerical order. The black cap is but a square covering of the round coif. According to ancient ecclesiastical casuistry, clerics being judges, handed over to the civil officers the duty of inflicting capital punishment. To the present day the bishops in the House of Lords do not take part in the criminal functions of that body.

41. "ESCALUS (to *Duke*). I have laboured for the poor gentle-man [Claudio] to the utmost shore of my modesty; but my brother justice [Angelo] I have found so severe, that he has forced me to tell him, he is indeed *justice*."

In order to remove a platitude we may suppose a legal pun, "So severe,"—he is indeed *just-ice*.

ACT IV., SCENE 2.

42. " POMPEY (to *Abhorson*, the hangman). Pray, Sir, by your
good favour,—do you call, Sir, your occupation a *mystery?*
ABHORSON. Ay, Sir; a *mystery.*"

" Mystery," from the French *meistier*, *métier*, was an old legal
term for a trade or occupation. This appears from what follows:—

" ABHORSON (to *Pompey*). Come on, bawd; I will instruct
thee in my *trade.*"

The usual covenant by a master, in an indenture of apprenticeship
to teach his apprentice his " mystery," means to teach him his *trade*,
and not, as often is supposed, the secrets or tricks of his trade.

43. " POMPEY (to *Provost*). I do find your hangman is a more
penitent trade than your bawd; he doth oftener *ask forgiveness.*"

This refers to the custom of the executioner asking forgiveness of
the convict before putting him to death.

44. " ANGELO (in his Notice to the *Provost*). Then fail not to
do your office, as you will answer it at your peril."

This is in imitation of the legal phraseology used in English
judicial warrants.

SCENE 3.

45. " POMPEY. All great doers in our trade [*i.e.* of a bawd]
are now *for the Lord's sake.*"

Pompey had been describing various prisoners in custody, and
ends by saying, that they were "all for the Lord's sake." This
refers to a custom of prisoners letting down, by a string from their
prison window, a basket, to receive the alms of passers by, whom
they would move to pity by crying out, " For the Lord's sake."

SCENE 4.

46. "ANGELO.   He should have liv'd,
Save that his riotous youth, with dangerous sense,
Might in the times to come, have ta'en revenge,
By so *receiving* a dishonour'd life,
With ransom of such shame."

There is some obscurity in the wording of this passage. " Ransom "
is a legal term for a sum of money paid for pardoning some offence.
For " receiving a dishonoured life," we prefer to read, *reviving a
dishonoured life.*

The argument of *Angelo* seems to be, that if he allowed Claudio
to live, who had been put into possession of the fact of Angelo's
attempt on Isabella, that Claudio might seek revenge afterwards, by
extorting money from Angelo by threatening to *revive* [*i.e.*, make
public] the secret of his (Angelo's) "dishonoured life."

ACT V., SCENE 1.

47. " MARIANA (to *Duke*). I am *affianced* this man's wife."

She means, not that she had been married to him, but that a
private contract to marry had been made between them ; which
Mariana explains by adding, " as strongly as words can make up
vows," *i.e.*, without the publicity of marriage ceremonies. "Affianced,"
in law, is the simple plighting of troth between a man and a woman,
or an agreement to marry.

48. " DUKE (to *Isabella*).   Think'st thou, thy oaths,
Though they would *swear down each particular saint*,
Were testimonies against his worth and credit,
That's *scaled* in approbation."

" Scaled " seems to be used for *sealed*, as in a previous quotation.
The oaths of others were not to be of value as against Angelo, whose
words were *scaled*, *i.e.*, of a higher value, and in approbation.
To " swear down each particular saint" seems to refer to a custom

of running down a list of saints, and swearing by each in turn, as certain people pray to each saint in turn.

49.   " Duke.   You, Lord Escalus,
       Sit with my *cousin* [Angelo]."

The Duke here calls Lord Angelo his " cousin," following the English custom, by which peers are called *cousins* by the sovereign. For the same reason, probably, that Angelo was ranked as a peer, he had previously made his protestation of his innocence on his " honour," and not on his *oath*. The Lords deliver their judgments in a criminal matter on " honour" only.

50.   " Escalus (sitting as judge with *Angelo*).
       The Duke's *in us*, and we will hear you speak ;
       Look you, speak justly."

This follows a fiction of English law, already noticed, according to which the sovereign is supposed, though absent, to be present with the judges who administered justice in his name.

51.   " Duke (*disguised as a Friar*). His subject I am not ;
       Nor his *provincial*."

The Duke here appearing as a friar, denies that he is a subject of the Duke, or is " his provincial "—a term of ecclesiastical law, which is here applied to a supposed monk living within an ecclesiastical jurisdiction, called *a province*.

52.   " Angelo (to the *Duke*).   Thou good Prince,
       No longer *session hold* upon my shame,
       But let my *trial* be mine own *confession*."

" Session " means the *sitting* of a court of justice. Angelo wishes to be sentenced on his *own confession*, and to be spared a public trial and proof by witnesses.

53.   " Duke (to *Isabella*).   I am still
       Attorney'd at your service."

An " attorney " at law represented his client in court, and

managed the case in his absence. It is a good old English title, although that of *solicitor*, which would be the corresponding title in a suit in Chancery, is now affected. Our Lord is called an *attorney* in Wycliff's translation.

> 54.   "DUKE (to *Mariana*).   For his [Angelo's] possessions,
> Although by *confiscation* they are ours,
> We do instate, and *widow* you with all."

"Confiscation" refers to an old English law, by which, on conviction for certain crimes, the offender's possessions were confiscated to the Crown. For "widow" we prefer to read *endow*. "We do instate and endow you with all," *i.e.*, the Duke transferred the confiscated possession as a *dowry* to Mariana, the Duke adding, "to buy you a better husband." Good dowries attracted rich husbands.

> 55.   "LUCIO (to the *Duke*). Marrying a punk, my lord, is *pressing to death*, whipping, and hanging."

We have here a legal practice referred to, in "pressing to death." Formerly, if a prisoner would not plead to an indictment, heavy weights were piled upon his breast until he pleaded, or died under the pressure.

"ALL'S WELL THAT ENDS WELL."

Lord Campbell, from his published notes on this Play, seems to have discovered in it only a few proofs of Shakespeare's knowledge of law. They are such as show the Poet's acquaintance with some of the incidents of the military tenure of land, or "tenure in chivalry," which existed until the time of Charles II. On a closer examination of this Play, than that which was made by his Lordship, we detect very numerous proofs which point to the possession by the Poet of a large fund of legal erudition, although it is not so abundant as in *Measure for Measure*. This difference may, to some extent, be accounted for by the absence from it of scenes favourable to the introduction of legal knowledge.

All's Well that Ends Well has a peculiarity which fits it for our purpose of comment and correction. It has been noted that it has suffered more corruptions than any of the Plays which have been attributed to Shakespeare. The presence of legal arguments and law terms had been the sources of many misunderstandings to printers, and consequently of blunders; but many of such errors have been found capable, we conceive, of restoration to intelligibility.

ACT I., SCENE 1.

1. "COUNTESS (to *Bertram, her Son*). In *delivering* my son from me, I bury a second husband.

BERTRAM. And I, in going, madam, weep o'er my father's death anew; but I must attend his *Majesty's* command, to whom I am now in *ward, evermore* in subjection."

Formerly, English sovereigns held not only the possession of estates held *in capite* from the Crown during the minority of the heir to them, but also of the person of the heir himself; and they also claimed the right of disposing of him in marriage, whereby some maiden of the sovereign's choice might be enriched by an alliance with a wealthy bachelor.

The expression " in delivering my son," *i.e.*, as a ward to the king, is a legal phrase suitable to the occasion. There is evidently a mistake in " I am now a ward *evermore* in subjection ;" for the custody of the ward ceased on the ward's attaining his majority. We therefore prefer to read, *moreover in subjection, i.e.*, to his will.

2.   " COUNTESS (speaking of *Helena*). She *derives* her honesty, and *achieves* her goodness."

" She derives " is a legal term, meaning to take by descent from her father, answering to " her disposition she inherits," and is the antithesis to "achieves her goodness"—*i.e.*, it is the result of personal merit. Thus we read in " Twelfth Night " (Act II., Scene 5), " Some are born great, some achieve greatness, and some have greatness thrust upon them."

3.   " COUNTESS (to *her Son*).   And thy goodness
    Share with thy birthright."

Here "share" does not mean to be *divided with*, but means *equal to ;* as if the Countess had said, Let your share of your father's goodness be equal to your claim on his estate. In "Measure for Measure " (Act I., Scene 1), we read, " Goodness share with thy birthright."

4.   " PAROLLES (to *Helena*). He that hangs himself, is a virgin : Virginity *murders itself ;* and should be *buried in highways*, out of all sanctified limit."

This contains a reference to an old law, according to which the body of a person guilty of *felo-de-se*, or self-murder, was not buried in the churchyard, but in some cross-road.

5.   " PAROLLES (to *Helena*). Besides, virginity is the most *inhibited sin* in the *canon*."

" Inhibited " is a term in ecclesiastical law, and " canon " refers to the canonized Scriptures. But in 1 Tim. v. 14, by " women " understand " widows."

6.   " PAROLLES (to *Helena*). Within ten years it [virginity] will
make itself ten, which is a goodly increase; and the *principal*
itself not much the worse."

The reference here, is to the practice of lending money at interest.
The mother is compared to the " principal," and her children to the
interest.

SCENE 2.

7.   " KING (*describing Bertram's father*). Who were below him
He us'd as creatures *of another place*;
And bow'd his eminent top to their low ranks,
Making them proud *of* his humility."

The words " of another place" are vague.   The reference seems
to be to the distinction of legal ranks.   We should, therefore, prefer
to read, he used [*i.e.*, treated] as creatures of a *higher* place; thus
bringing out the antithesis to "their low ranks."   Instead of " making
them proud *of* his humility," it might be an improvement to read, *by
his humility*.

8.   " KING (*dangerously ill*).   Nature and sickness
Debate it at their *leisure*."

A happy metaphor borrowed from courts of law.   The life of the
patient is the subject *debated*.   There is, perhaps, in the phrase " at
their leisure," a sly hit at the prosiness of barristers.

SCENE 3.

9.   " CLOWN (to *his mistress*). *Service* is no *heritage*."

The clown is desiring the Countess's permission to marry, and he
intimates that though his father had been a serf of the family, yet
that serfdom had ceased, and that therefore *he* was free to marry
as he pleased.

10. " COUNTESS (speaking of *Helena* to her *Steward*). Her father

bequeathed her to me ; and she herself, without other *advantage*, may *lawfully make title* to as much love as she finds."

That is : Helena's father had by his *will* appointed or " bequeathed " his daughter to be a *ward* of the Countess ; and, although he had left no property with her, still Helena might lawfully look for the love of the Countess, as being her guardian. " To make title to" is a legal phrase.

11.   " COUNTESS. It is the *shew* and *seal* of nature's truth,
Where love's strong passion is *impressed in* youth."

Supposing that Shakespeare had engaged in law, we think it not improbable that he wrote, referring to deeds :—

It is the *sign* and *seal* of nature's truth,
When love's strong passion is impressed *on* youth.

12.   " COUNTESS (to *Helena*). Come, come, disclose
The state of your affections ; for your passions
Have to the full *appeached*."

For " appeached" we should probably use the legal term *impeached*. " Appeached " is not elsewhere found in Shakespeare, although he elsewhere uses *impeached*. (Merchant of Venice, Act III., Scenes 2 & 3 ; Henry VI., Scenes 1 & 4).

13.   " HELENA. Whose aged honour *cites* a virtuous youth."

" To cite " does not here mean to *quote*, but it stands probably for *recites*. " To recite," in law, means to set forth in a document certain antecedents preliminary to a result. " Aged honour" is assumed to have been *preceded* by " a virtuous youth."

ACT II., SCENE 1.

14.   " KING (to a *Lord*).   Let higher Italy
(Those *bated*, that *inherit but* the fall
Of the last monarchy) see that you come," &c.

The application of a little law will bring sense out of these obscure lines. To "bate," or abate, has the special legal meaning, not merely of putting out of possession, but the putting out of a wrongful possessor, in favour of a legal claimant. For "inherit *but* the fall," we propose to read *inherit by the fall.* The parenthesis will then stand—Those wrongful possessors being abated, or turned out of possession, who took possession on the fall of the last monarchy.

15. " 1st Lord. There's honour in the theft.
    Parolles.   Commit it, Count.
    2nd Lord. I am your *accessory.*"

An "accessory" in law is a party not actually guilty of a crime as a principal, but yet punishable for assisting in its commission. The 2nd Lord, by his speech, would thus encourage the Count to commit the theft by assuming to himself a liability to punishment for it.

16. " King. When our most learned doctors leave us; and
    The *congregated College* have concluded
    That," &c.

The reference is here to a legal charter first granted by Edward VI. to the then formed College of Physicians.

Scene 2.

17. " Clown. As fit as ten groats *is* for the hand of an *Attorney.*"

Shakespeare knew that an attorney's fee was 3s. 4d. The singular " is " shows that there was a coin then current worth 10 groats.

Scene 3.

18. " Lafeu. To be relinquished of the artists.
    Parolles. So I say; both of Galen and Paracelsus.
    Lafeu. Of all the learned and *authentic fellows*, that gave him up as incurable."

Here there is a second reference to the then new College of

Physicians. " Authentic fellows," *i.e.*, the fellows entitled legally under its provisions to practise medicine.

19.   " KING (to *Helena*). Fair maid, send forth thine eye;
       this youthful *parcel*
   Of noble bachelors stand at my bestowing."

These "noble bachelors" were wards of the King, and whom, therefore, he might bestow in marriage at his will. This was formerly the law of England. The phrase " this youthful parcel " is not dignified. Perhaps we should read *this youthful panel*, a law term applied to the row of jurors arranged in court.

20.   " KING (speaking of *Helena*). She is young, wise, fair;
   In these to *Nature* she's *immediate heir*,—
   I can *create* the rest : *virtue and she*
   Is her own dower; *honour* and wealth from me."

Here several legal ideas and terms are introduced in accordance with English law.

" Immediate heir," not collateral, so that she had her virtues from her father. " Create," a legal term applied to the conferring of titles by the sovereign. "Dower," what the maid brought to her husband on their marriage. For " virtue and she," we prefer to read, conjecturally, *virtue*—virtue has she as her own dower; thereby correcting grammar.

21.   " KING (to *Bertram*). Thou dost in vile *misprison* shackle up
   My love, and her desert."

" Misprison " is a law term derived from the French word *mépris*, *i.e.*, contempt. It is applied to contempt of authority, and is, therefore, here most apposite.

22.   " KING (to *Bertram*). Good fortune, and the favour of the
       king,
   Smile upon this *contract; whose ceremony*
   Shall seem expedient on this new-born *brief*
   And be performed to night ; the solemn feast

> Shall *more* attend upon the coming *space*,
> Expecting absent friends. As thou lov'st her,
> Thy love's to *me religious ;* else, does err."

This speech is manifestly corrupt. A few alterations and legal explanations may tend to restore it to its original form.

The Poet regards marriage from a purely legal point of view when he describes it as a " contract ; " which it is, in the eye of the law. By "religious," in connection with "love," is meant a public religious celebration, not by *private contract*. By "coming state," a reference is made to the title to be conferred on Helena by the King.

We propose to alter the lines thus :—

> Good fortune, and the favour of the King,
> Smile upon this contráct. *Such* like ceremony
> *As* seems expedient on this new-born *love*
> *Shall* be performed to-night. The solemn feast
> Shall *soon* attend upon the coming *state*,
> Expecting absent friends. As thou lov'st her,
> Thy love's to *be* religious ; else does err.

23.   " LAFEU. By mine honour, if I were but two hours younger, I'd *beat* thee ; methinks thou art a *general offence*, and every man should *beat* thee."

A slight alteration and a legal explanation will bring out the point of these lines. For "beat" we would read *abate*, which is a legal term, meaning to remove a nuisance. By " general offence" is meant a *public nuisance*, which any person might by law abate or remove. This is one of the two ancient legal rights of the time when men were free to protect themselves. Anyone, without evoking the aid of a constable, may remove a nuisance from a public road ; and every landlord may help himself to his tenant's goods for rent in arrear.

Scene 5.

24.   " LAFEU. You have it from his own *deliverance*.
BERTRAM. And by other *warranted testimony*."

D

"Deliverance," in law, means *a declaring*. The jury on a criminal trial are sworn to make a true deliverance, *i.e.*, to *deliver* a true verdict. It seems to be unwise still to retain, in the common oath of jurymen, a word which common jurymen would rarely understand. For "warranted testimony" it would probably be better to read *warranting testimony*.

> 25.   "PAROLLES (to *Lafeu*). I know not how I have deserved to run into my lord's displeasure.
>
>   LAFEU. You have made shift to run into't;—and out of it you'll run again, rather than *suffer question* for your residence."

To "suffer question" seems to refer to questioning by torture, *i.e.*, to be severely punished if he refused to go away.

ACT III., SCENE 2.

> 26.   "CLOWN. I knew a man that had a trick of melancholy, *hold* a goodly manor for a song."

Manors were sometimes granted by kings to be held by the payment of very frivolous services ; but such a tenure is not referred to by the clown. We therefore prefer to read, *sold a goodly manor for a song*.

SCENE 4.

> 27.   "COUNTESS (to *Steward*).   He cannot thrive,
> Unless her prayers, whom Heaven delights to hear,
> And loves to grant, *reprieve* him from the
> Wrath of *greatest* justice.".

"Reprieve" is a legal term, from the French *repris*, and subsequently passed into common use. It means the suspended execution of punishment For "greatest justice" we should probably read *strictest justice;* for justice scarcely admits of degrees, but the infliction of its penalties may.

ACT IV., SCENE 2.

28. "DIANA (to *Bertram*). Ay, so you serve us,
Till we serve you; but when you have our roses,
You barely [q. basely] leave our thorns to prick ourselves,
And mock us with our bareness [q. baseness].
BERTRAM (to *Diana*). How have I sworn!
DIANA. 'Tis not the many oaths that make the truth,
But the plain single vow, that is vowed true.
What is not holy, that we swear not by,
But take the Highest to witness. Then, pray you, tell me,
If I should swear by Jove's great attributes,
I lov'd you dearly, would you believe my oaths,
When I did love you ill? This has no holding,
To swear by him whom I protest to love,
That I will work against him ; therefore your oaths
Are words, and poor conditions ; but unsealed,—
At least in my opinion."

These lines are full of reference to legal matters. We find *sworn*,
vowed, conditions, and *unsealed.* It will be difficult to trace the course
of argument introduced, until some one can ingeniously restore the
passage from evident corruptions.

29. "DIANA (to *Bertram*). Thus your own proper wisdom
Brings in the *champion, Honour*, on my part,
Against your vain *assault.*"

" A champion " was, in ancient law, a person who fought on behalf
of another in a trial by combat—a mode of decision which was a few
years since abolished by Act of Parliament.

SCENE 3.

30. "1ST LORD. Now, God delay our *rebellion ;* as we are
ourselves, what things are we ? "

This prayer, " God delay our rebellion," is devoid of meaning.

Bertram's seduction of Diana had just been spoken of,—the Lord
who had been a party to it might therefore say, Now God delay our
retribution.

    31.   " 1st LORD. Her death was faithfully confirmed by the
    rector of the place."

In England the "rector" of parish, or other incumbent, kept
registers of burials and gave certificates of burials, to be used as
evidence.

    32.   " 2ND LORD. Hath the Count all this intelligence?
           1st LORD. Ay,—and the particular confirmations, point
from point, to the full *arming* of the verity."

For "arming" we prefer to read *arraying of the verity;* for to
array is an old legal term signifying to *set forth in order.*

    33.   " BERTRAM. I have to-night despatched sixteen businesses,
    a month's length apiece, by an *abstract* of *success.*"

" An abstract of success " can be best explained by referring to
the law. " An abstract" means an *abridgement;* and as to " success,"
it is elsewhere used by Shakespeare for *succession;* so that this
obscure phrase may mean *in quick succession.*

    34.   " 1st SOLDIER (to *Parolles*). Shall I set down your answer
    so ?
           PAROLLES. Do ; I'll *take the sacrament* on 't, how and
which way you will."

There is here a reference to an old solemn form of taking an
oath. Sometimes a person was to be sworn on the host, as here ;
sometimes on the relics of saints, as Harold is said to have sworn to
William ; and, as now, men swear over the Gospels by kissing the
book.

    35.   " PAROLLES. Sir, for a *quart d'ecu* he will sell the *fee simple*

of his salvation, the *inheritance* of it; and *cut the entail* from *all remainders*, and a *perpetual succession* for it *perpetually*."

Here is a crop of legal phraseology, and the idea intended to be conveyed is clear; but as Shakespeare is putting law terms into the mouth of a layman, he, as usual, salts them with blunders. The reference is to an estate held in fee, in tail, and in mortmain.

SCENE 4.

36. " HELENA (to *Widow*). Doubt not, but Heaven
Hath brought me up *to be your daughter's dower*,
As it hath been fated her to be my motive
And helper to a husband."

Helena means, by "to be your daughter's dower," that by the accomplishment of the plan in which the daughter had been the "motive," *i.e.*, a *means* in joining a husband to Helena (*Vide* Othello, Act IV., Scene 2), she, Helena, would be enabled to provide a dower or dowry for the daughter's own marriage.

SCENE 5.

37. " COUNTESS (to *Lafeu*). My lord, that's gone, made himself much sport out of him [the *Clown*]: by his authority he remains here, which he thinks is a *patent* for his sauciness; and, indeed, he has no *pace*, but runs where he will."

For " pace " we should read *place*. The reference would then be to the law of letters patent, by which a sovereign conferred *place* and duty.

38. " LAFEU (to the *Countess*). Madame, I was thinking with what manners I might safely be admitted [*i.e.*, to the presence of the King].
" COUNTESS. You need but plead your *honourable privilege*.
" LAFEU. Of that I have made a *bold charter*; but, I thank my God, it holds yet."

By " your honourable privilege " is probably meant the right of
a peer (and such Lafeu was) to have at any time an audience with
his sovereign.   But what is meant by "a bold charter?"   May it
refer to *bed-chamber*, and to the high office of *chamberlain*, the holder
of which office would have ever ready access to the King ?

Act V., Scene 2.

39.   " Lafeu (to *Parolles*, begging alms of him).   There's a
quart d'écu for you; but the *justices* make you and fortune
friends."

The reference is to the Poor Law, by which Justices of the Peace
had to grant a pauper's maintenance.

Scene 3.

40.   " Bertram (to *Lafeu*). Noble she was, and thought
        I stood ingag'd; but when I had *subscrib'd*
        To mine own fortune, and inform'd her fully,
        I could not answer in that course of honour
        As she had made the overture, she ceas'd,
        In heavy satisfaction, and would never
        Receive the ring again."

There are obscurities in this passage.   The following emendations
may perhaps be accepted.   Instead of " I had subscribed to mine
own fortune," read, *I had described to her my fortune*.   And instead
of " In heavy satisfaction," read, *on having satisfaction*, which was
originally a legal expression.

Lawyers speak of *entering satisfaction* on a *judgment* against a
party.

41.   " King (to *Bertram*). She call'd the saints to *surety*,
        That she would never put it from her finger,
        Unless," &c.

" Surety" is a legal term, standing for *bail*, or parties bound on
behalf of another.

42. " LAFEU. I will *buy* me a son-in-law in a *fair*, and *toll* ; for this, I'll none of him."

An old law can most easily explain this passage. If a beast were purchased in a *market ouvert*, and such was a *fair*, and the *toll* due thereon was paid, a purchase so made was good against all the world, even though the beast had been previously stolen. We should therefore prefer to read—I will *buy* me a son-in-law in a *fair*, and pay *toll:* for this,—I'll none of him. Lafeu had expected to have got Bertram for his son-in-law, and it had been fully arranged, when his expectations are blasted by the re-appearance of Helena, who claims Bertram for herself. Lafeu means that he will take care not to be ever so let in again. Who but a lawyer would have introduced an analogy from such a source ?

43. " DIANA (accused, to the *King*). I'll put in *bail*, my liege.
Good mother, fetch my *bail*.
The *jeweller*, that owes [owns] the ring, is sent for,
And he shall *surety* me."

The quick-witted Diana, having been threatened to be sent to prison, and knowing her innocence, talks as if she were well acquainted with the law of *bail*, or *suretyship*. " Jewellers" were formerly the only bankers, and being, therefore, considered wealthy, were unexceptionable bail.

We have thus completed a closer examination of two of Shakespeare's Plays, " Measure for Measure" and " All's Well that Ends Well," than that which they had received from Lord Campbell. In the first of these Plays we have detected fifty-five, and in the second forty-three passages, which supply evidence, more or less suggestive, of Shakespeare's being well acquainted with English law ; and not only so, but they prove that his thoughts were, as a practitioner's, full of it. In addition, we have attempted to throw light on many

obscure speeches, and to correct many apparently corrupt words and
phrases, by bringing them under a legal focus. In our examination
of the two Plays we have met with many other legal terms, but to
which we have not called attention, *e.g.*, proclamation, peculiar fel-
lowship, under penalty, convented, infringe, vouch, disvouch, tender
down, quests, &c.

Such is the amount of legal lore displayed by Shakespeare in the
two Plays, that we have been driven to the conclusion that he must
have been practically acquainted with English law, and, therefore,
that the seven years in his early life, which his biographers have
been unable to account for, were spent in an attorney's office at
Stratford. He was not a mere dabbler in picked-up law. He never
lays down bad law, except intentionally, when the speakers are not
professional men; and then there is an evident intention of throwing
ridicule on such pretenders to legal knowledge. Shakespeare must
have been an adept in English law, or he would not have ventured
to show up a pretentious ignorance of it in others.

There is one test which might be applied as to the correctness of
the conclusion at which we have arrived as to Shakespeare's knowledge of law. Let the plays of the dramatists who preceded, or
were contemporary with him, be examined, and if they are not so
full of legal knowledge as Shakespeare's, the question, Why not?
will remain to be answered.

It may be objected, that in several of Shakespeare's Plays there is
not the same manifest exuberance of a legal mind as in the two
which have now been examined. This may be true; but, as a
negative argument, it avails but little against the positive evidence
deduced from two of his Plays. Nor is the doubt in which Lord
Campbell left the question which was before him of much moment;
for if his cursory examination had been extended to the gathering
together of *all* the evidence which lay unrecognized before him, his
conclusion would probably have raised the Poet to at least an
honorary membership of his own learned profession.

Our Great Dramatist has been rarely criticized by a member of
the legal profession. It were, therefore, much to be desired that
some competent lawyers, moved by a spirit of reverence towards his

memory, and feeling within themselves critical instincts and the power of patiently kneeling before doubts, should set themselves to study attentively, and to cleanse lovingly one of the noblest, and, as we think, one of the most defaced monuments of genius in existence; and so wipe away the spots which, though many of them are small, yet in fact are almost innumerable, are hiding, like a veil, the object of all praise. Then would they turn that honour, which with the many is now but a blind superstition, into an open-eyed appreciation of the Poet's works.

There was a time when the early printed texts of Shakespeare's Plays were regarded with such reverence that the critics strained their art to justify what was unjustifiable. But a change has come Instead of now assuming the correctness of the early texts, and thereby heaping on the Poet's fame the grossest charges of incapacity and carelessness, it is assumed, both wisely and justly, that the printers of his Plays were wrong; and we know that the Poet had nothing to do with them. It has often been a matter of wonderment with students of the Plays how the innumerable errors and gross absurdities, which are patent on the early texts, could have crept into existence. The only solution which we suggest is this: That the printers first employed in England were from Germany (where the printing art was born), and that they were but imperfectly acquainted with the English tongue, and therefore innocent of a legal capacity of knowing whether they were printing sense or not.

PRINTED BY WITHERBY & CO., MIDDLE ROW PLACE, HOLBORN.

ANNE BOLEYN. A Tragedy.

" Vigorous and polished."—*Observer.*

" Some really good passages in it; it indicates throughout an elegant and cultivated mind."—*Illustrated Weekly News.*

" Powerful blank verse, sound principles, and poetic feeling."—*Western Times.*

Price 5s.

KENT & CO.

ON THE USE OF JEHOVAH AND ELOHIM IN THE PENTATEUCH, AS CONSISTENT WITH AND CONFIRMATORY OF ITS MOSAIC AUTHORSHIP.

" A remarkable book. We think that the premises may be considered as in a high degree correct."—*Cambridge University Chronicle.*

" There is considerable merit in this brief treatise."—*Westminster Review.*

Price 2s. 6d.

LONGMANS & CO.

Preparing for Publication.

ON THE GENUINENESS AND MOSAIC AUTHORSHIP OF THE PENTATEUCH CONSIDERED AS A LAW-BOOK.

www.ingramcontent.com/pod-product-compliance
Lightning Source LLC
Chambersburg PA
CBHW022205020726
47496CB00008B/2884